The InSOMNIACS

KARINA WOLF

ILLUSTRATED BY
THE BROTHERS HILTS

G. P. Putnam's Sons • An Imprint of Penguin Group (USA) Inc.

G. P. PUTNAM'S SONS • A division of Penguin Young Readers Group.
Published by The Penguin Group.
Penguin Group (USA) Inc., 375 Hudson Street, New York, NY 10014, U.S.A.
Penguin Group (Canada), 90 Eglinton Avenue East, Suite 700, Toronto, Ontario M4P 2Y3, Canada
(a division of Pearson Penguin Canada Inc.).
Penguin Books Ltd, 80 Strand, London WC2R 0RL, England.
Penguin Ireland, 25 St. Stephen's Green, Dublin 2, Ireland (a division of Penguin Books Ltd.).
Penguin Group (Australia), 250 Camberwell Road, Camberwell, Victoria 3124, Australia
(a division of Pearson Australia Group Pty Ltd).
Penguin Books India Pvt Ltd, 11 Community Centre, Panchsheel Park, New Delhi - 110 017, India.
Penguin Group (NZ), 67 Apollo Drive, Rosedale, Auckland 0632, New Zealand (a division of Pearson New Zealand Ltd).
Penguin Books (South Africa) (Pty) Ltd, 24 Sturdee Avenue, Rosebank, Johannesburg 2196, South Africa.
Penguin Books Ltd, Registered Offices: 80 Strand, London WC2R 0RL, England.

Design by Marikka Tamura.
Text set in Lo-Type Light.
The art was created using pencil, charcoal and a computer.
Library of Congress Cataloging-in-Publication Data
Wolf, Karina.
The Insomniacs / Karina Wolf ; illustrated by The Brothers Hilts [i.e. Sean and Ben Hilts].   p. cm.
Summary: When Mr. and Mrs. Insomniac and little Mika move twelve time zones away,
they have trouble staying awake during the day and make an interesting discovery about themselves.
[1. Sleep—Fiction.] I. Hilts, Ben, ill. II. Hilts, Sean, ill. III. Title.
PZ7.W81918In 2012   [E]—dc23   2011028760
ISBN 978-0-399-25665-3
3 5 7 9 10 8 6 4 2

For my mom and dad, Elizabeth and Aaron—K.W.

For Pop, Carisa, Kate and Lex—S & B

$\mathcal{T}$he Insomniacs weren't always a night family.

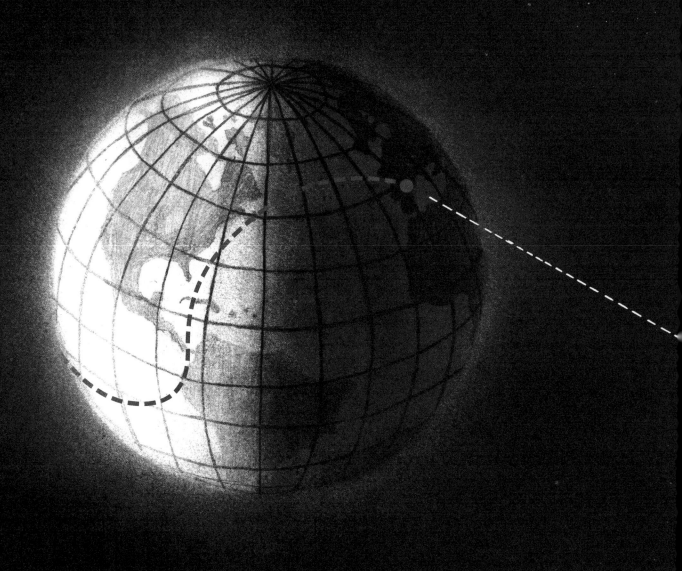

But when Mrs. Insomniac found a new job,
Mother, Father, and little Mika traveled twelve
time zones to their new home.

When they arrived, they found they stayed awake only in the nighttime.

At sunup, they yawned and stretched. They were ready for an eight-hour rest.

Mother dragged herself to work
and nodded at her desk.

Father took pictures at his studio
and then took forty winks.

Mika listened to her lessons but sleepwalked through the science lab.

The headmistress sent her home with a note.

"I suspect Mika has sleeping sickness. Please see a specialist right away!"

"This won't do," said little Mika. "We have to sleep at night."

That evening, the Insomniacs took hot baths,
filled the crossword, pulled down the shades
and pulled up the covers.

Mika counted to one thousand.

Father sipped six mugs of milk.

Mother tried a meditation—as suggested for
her star sign in the evening paper.

But by 3:00 A.M. they found themselves awake again.
"Nothing helps!" cried little Mika. "It's tiresome waking
all night long."

"Let's have a family huddle," said Mother.
And they puzzled over their shut-eye trouble.

"Who rests the longest and the best?" said
Mrs. Insomniac. "I wonder if our neighbors
have better luck with bedtime."

"We don't have neighbors," said Mika meekly.

"Not true," said Father. He pointed to the darkness beyond the windowpane. "Lynx take catnaps. Reindeer stand up."

"And walrus drowse with one eye open," added Mother.

"But bears bed down all winter long!" said Mika. "We'll find the bears and ask them for their slumber secrets."

So, in search of bears,

the Insomniacs trekked

beyond the house,

through the pines,

into the cliffs . . .

and found a cave.

But there weren't any bears.
Instead, they saw a horde of mice
hanging upside down.

The cloud of animals roused and rushed
into the night.
They weren't mice at all.
They dipped and dived and surfed the air.
They squealed with delight.

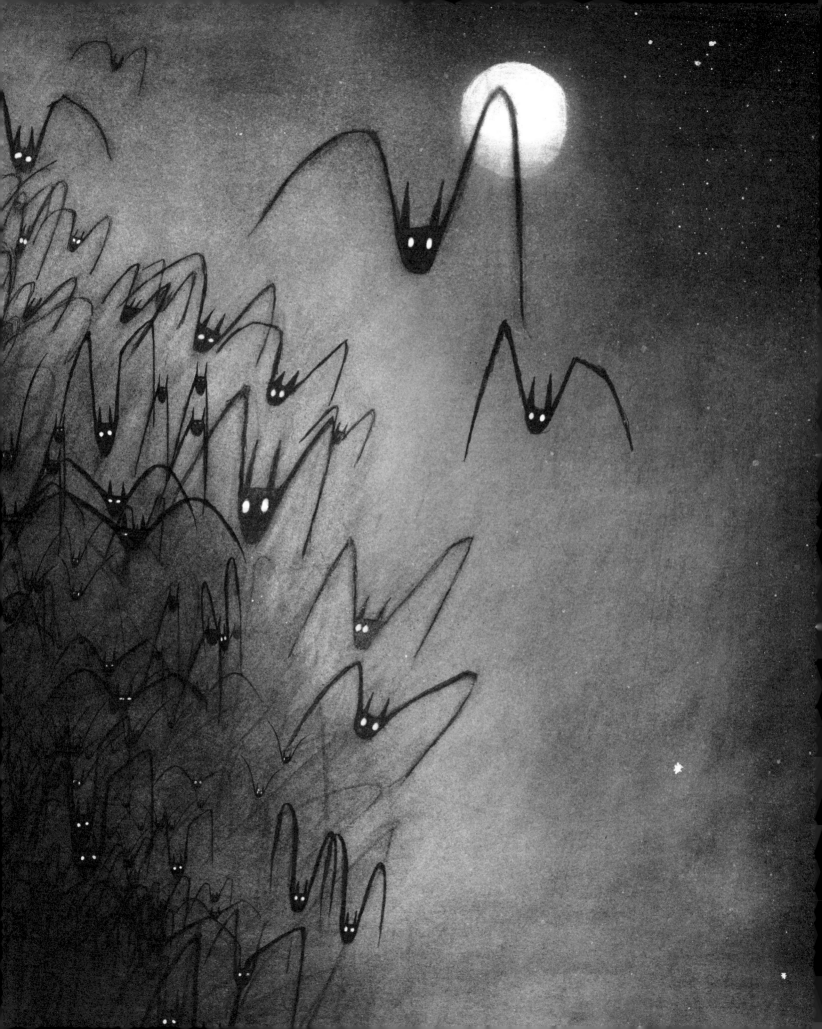

And then the Insomniacs noticed: the darkness was full of life.

"Why don't *we* give night a try?" said little Mika.
The Insomniacs decided to live during the dark hours.

At dusk, they woke and ate a breakfast
of nightshade vegetables.
They dressed in midnight blue.

When the moon rose,
Mother tended a moonlight cactus
and Father watched the evening news.

Mika wrangled her nighttime pets—an aardvark, an angel shark,
a bandicoot and a small-eared zorro frisked in Mika's room.
A fennec fox lived under her bed, and she fed him night beetles.

The planets wheeled around the sky while
the Insomniacs toiled in the gloom.

Father developed his photos in a darkroom.
Mother studied stars through her telescope,
and Mika attended night school remotely.

And after work, they moonbathed and watched
the fishes nipping at the surface of the sea.
They went to the flower market and to the bakery,
where the dough rose with the sun.

They returned
home on the
quiet streets.

They put away their groceries and their flowers.

At dawn, they went to sleep.

They adored their new life.

Every now and then, sunlight crept through the blinds and climbed the walls and reminded the Insomniacs of daytime.

They opened the door and looked at the sun's glare that bleached the world out there.

The dazzle made them blink and sigh and rub their eyes.

"I much prefer the night," said Mika.

The Insomniacs didn't need the sun;
they had stars and fireflies and northern lights.
"We are a nighttime family," they all agreed.
They shuttered out the morning sky
and bundled into bed.